Mum's the Word

**Michael Morpurgo
and Shoo Rayner**

Collins

For Mike Plant
and everyone at Treginnis

This edition produced for The Book People Ltd
Hall Wood Avenue, Haydock
St Helens WA11 9UL

Published by A & C Black in 1995
Published by Collins in 1996
10 9 8 7 6 5 4 3
Collins is an imprint of HarperCollins*Publishers* Ltd,
77-85 Fulham Palace Road, Hammersmith, London W6 8JB.

ISBN 0 00 763096 4

Text © 1995 Michael Murpurgo
Illustrations © 1995 Shoo Rayner

Michael Murpurgo and Shoo Rayner assert the moral right to be identified as the author and the
illustrator of the work.
A CIP record for this title is available from the British Library.

Printed and bound in Great Britain by
Omnia Books Limited, Glasgow

Chapter One

There was once a family of all sorts
of animals that lived in the
farmyard behind the tumbledown
barn on Mudpuddle Farm.

You are the sunshine of my life...

At
first
light every
morning
Frederick, the
flame-feathered
cockerel, lifted
his eyes to the sun
and crowed and crowed
until the light came on in old
Farmer Rafferty's bedroom window.

One . . . . by . . . . one,
the animals crept out into the dawn . . .

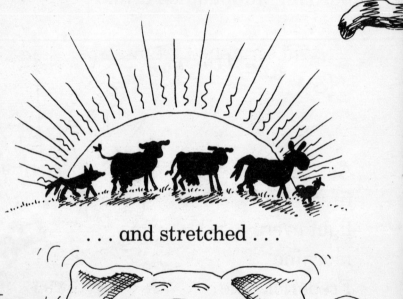

. . . and stretched . . .

. . . and yawned . . .

. . . and scratched themselves.

But no-one ever spoke a word, not until after breakfast.

One morning, Captain was crunching away at his last mouthful of breakfast hay when he noticed something was wrong.

Someone was missing. Gone!

Albertine and her little goslings were preening themselves on their island.

Upside and Down
were upside down
in the pond.

Peggoty and her little piglets,
including Pintsize, snuffled and
snorted around the dungheap.

Diana the silly sheep who couldn't
count to save her life, was counting
the clouds.

Penelope and her chicks scratched and scuffled in the orchard, never too far from Frederick.

Grace and Primrose grazed nose to nose in the meadow.

Jigger, the almost always sensible sheepdog, was chasing his tail again.

And Mossop, the cat with the one and single eye, was curled up asleep on his tractor seat as he always was.

BUT, where was Egbert the grumbly goat?

Jigger, have you seen that grumbly goat?

Nope, I'll have a look shall I?

So Jigger looked and looked.

But Egbert wasn't eating paint off the gate....

Egbert wasn't anywhere. He'd done
a bunk, buzzed off, gone walkabout.

If anyone knows where he is,
thought Jigger, Albertine will,
because Albertine always knows
everything. So Jigger ran down to
the pond.

Albertine, have you *seen* Egbert anywhere? He seems to have gone *missing*.

But Egbert did not come back. The animals searched here, there and everywhere for him.

But it was no good, he couldn't
find him anywhere. No-one could
find him.

'I can't think where he's gone,' said
Grace, the dreamy-eyed brown cow.
'Nor me,' said Primrose, who
always agreed with her.

I don't know
where he's gone
either.

'I know, I know,'
said Diana, the
silly sheep.

He's gone
missing!

'Don't worry,' Albertine told her
little goslings.

That goat will be
back, you'll see, around
suppertime I should think.

she's so
reassuring.

Chapter Two

Sure enough, just as Old Farmer Rafferty was giving all the animals their supper that evening, Egbert wandered into the yard, grumbling as usual.

'Egbert, where have you been?' asked
Farmer Rafferty in the nasty, raspy
voice he kept for special occasions.

'Worried sick we were,' said
Captain, the cart-horse that
everyone loved and who loved
everyone.

But Egbert wouldn't say another word about it.

Down on her island in the pond,
Albertine shook her head, smiled
her goosey smile and thought deep
goosey thoughts.

I told you he'd come back, didn't
I? I'll tell you something else too,
just so long as you keep mum,
if you know what I mean. That
goat's been up to something.

what? What? What?

Who knows? Who knows?
Now, let's watch the sun go
down, and then we'll all go to sleep.

Chapter Three

It wasn't long after this that Egbert began behaving very strangely indeed. For one thing, he stopped grumbling. Everyone thought he must be sick, but he wasn't.

Are you feeling all right, Egbert?

Enigmatic Smile

'Good morning,' he'd say as he
passed by,

And he'd say that with the wind
whistling through the farmyard and
the rain thundering down on the
corrugated roofs.

Then one day, Diana the silly sheep
saw something very, very strange.
She saw Egbert dancing! And he
was singing too!

la... la la la... la la

Of course none of the animals
believed her at first, because Diana
was always silly. But she told them
and told them until they had to
come and look.

And of course, when they saw it
with their own eyes they had to
believe it. Egbert was dancing in the
puddles, and singing his heart out.

'He's really sick,'
said Jigger sadly.

'Hope it's not catching,' said
Penelope, hurrying her chicks away.

'He's gone loopy if you ask me,' said
Peggoty, keeping her distance at the
top of the dungheap.

Mossop opened his one and single
eye and shut it again.

I'm having a bad dream about a singing, dancing goat that's lost his marbles. I think he ought to see a vet.

But Grace and Primrose liked the song so much that they found a puddle of their own and joined in.

Albertine sighed and smiled secretly to herself.

'You'd never understand, Captain,' said Albertine; and Captain felt very stupid.

It'll be carrots next, or apples.... sometimes it's both.

Captain couldn't understand what Albertine was talking about, but he didn't want to say so in case she might think he was as stupid as he felt he was.

Chapter Four

It was Tuesday, and Tuesday was always the day Old Farmer Rafferty went off to market.

He put on his best jacket and his best hat. Then he scooped Mossop off his tractor seat and drove to market.

Off he went, happy as a lark,
singing to himself as he always did
when he was happy though he could
never remember the words.

But Old Farmer Rafferty had
forgotten something else, too.
Something much more important
than the words. He had forgotten to
close his vegetable garden gate.

Later that morning, Egbert was feeling even hungrier than usual.

Then he saw Farmer Rafferty's garden gate swinging in the wind, squeaking on its hinges.

'Carrots,' he thought. 'Apples.'

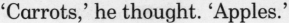

No-one saw
him tippy-toeing
out of the farmyard
except Mossop, who
happened to open his one
and single eye as Egbert passed by.

My goat dream again, only now he's on his tippy-toes and ballet dancing!

And he went back to sleep to finish
his dream.

All morning long, Egbert chomped
and chewed his way through Old
Farmer Rafferty's carrots. No-one
noticed what he was up to until
after lunch.

Early in the afternoon, Peggoty was
taking her piglets for a stroll. As
usual Pintsize had run on ahead.
That was why he reached the garden
gate first. Pintsize knew, and all the
animals knew, that none of them
(except Mossop because he was
special), was ever allowed inside Old
Farmer Rafferty's vegetable garden.

So when he saw Egbert standing in the middle of the vegetable garden with a carrot in his mouth, he knew that there was going to be trouble, big trouble.

Errk!

Pintsize loved it when other people
got into trouble for a change.

Mama!
Egbert is in
Mr Rafferty's
vegetable garden.
He's eaten all
the carrots!

Peggoty could not believe her eyes.
There wasn't a single carrot left
except the one in Egbert's mouth.

Is something the matter, Peggoty?

The little piglets gasped. Peggoty let
out her screechiest scream and
called for help.

Captain! Jigger! Albertine! Come quick, Come quick!

And all the animals came running
as fast as they could.

What's the matter?

'Egbert!' cried Captain. 'Out of there! Out of there! If Old Farmer Rafferty catches you in his vegetable garden your goose will be cooked!' And then he thought about what he'd said.

But Albertine just smiled.

But Captain still didn't understand.

'I'll get him out,' said Jigger, the almost always sensible sheepdog. He dashed into the garden and tried to pull Egbert out by his rope. But Egbert would not budge.

Captain came in to help as well but still Egbert dug his heels in and would not move.

In fact, Old Farmer Rafferty was
just at the end of the farm lane,
talking to Farmer Farley from the
next door farm. 'Goats,' Farmer
Farley was saying, 'who'd have
them? They go where they want, eat
what they want, do as they please.
Still they make you laugh don't
they?' And the two of them just
laughed and laughed.

Back in the farmyard, the animals
all heard Farmer Rafferty coming
up the lane on his tractor. He was
still singing away.

42

'I'm off,' said Jigger.

'Me too,' said Captain.

But Albertine decided to wait.
'I think I'll just stay and see what
happens,' she said.

Pintsize hid under Albertine's wings
and pretended to be a gosling.

As Old Farmer Rafferty came through the garden gate, all the animals hid behind the wall and watched.

Suddenly, Old Farmer Rafferty stopped singing. With bated breath, the animals waited for him to shout in his nasty, raspy voice. But he didn't.

All he said was:

You silly old goat, eating all my lovely carrots. Still, I expect you need them more than I do.

And Farmer Rafferty laughed and laughed. He picked up Egbert's rope and led him out into the orchard.

You have all the apples you can find my dear. You'll get fat, but that doesn't matter does it? You eat as much as you like.

The animals could not believe their ears. They could not understand it at all. But Albertine could. She smiled her goosey smile and waddled off back to her pond. Then she climbed up on to her island and tucked her head under her wing and slept. There were four little goslings under her wing that night, and one of them had trotters.

Chapter Five

It turned out just as Old Farmer Rafferty had said. Egbert did get fat, very fat. It wasn't surprising – he did nothing but eat all day long.

He ate anything and everything –

Captain's
best hay,

Jigger's
biscuits,

Peggoty's
pigmeal,

Penelope's
corn,

Diana's
sheepnuts,

and Old Farmer Rafferty's socks off
the washing line.

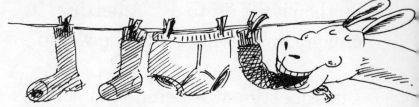

He even ate the sack that Mossop
used for his bed on the tractor seat.
'I'm not dreaming this,' said
Mossop, yawning hugely. 'That goat
is eating my bed.' Mossop was not
at all happy about that.

Right, that's the last straw.
What are we going to do
about that goat?

No-one knew what to do, but they all knew something had to be done. So they went off to ask Albertine. If anyone knew what to do she would.

But Albertine was being very secretive. 'Mum's the word,' she said inscrutably, and she would say no more.

'Well I think that goat needs to lose some weight,' said Grace, the dreamy-eyed brown cow.

And I agree. He's almost as fat as we are, and we are cows. We're supposed to be fat.

But how do you get thin if you're fat?

'Jogging,' said Jigger.

So five times a day all the animals, except Albertine who thought it was all very silly, jogged round Front Meadow. Afterwards they did their aerobics, and all the while Egbert would sing along quite happily.

'I'm singing in the sun, singing in the sun,' (or rain, depending on the weather). He didn't seem to mind the exercise at all, just so long as he could carry on eating afterwards.

And that's just what he did. He got fatter,

and fatter,

and fatter.

And to everyone's amazement, he stopped grumbling completely. The animals could not believe it.

'I'm just the happiest, luckiest goat in the whole wide world,' he said jumping into another puddle.

'What's he got to be so happy about?' said Jigger. 'What's happened to him?' And he went to ask Albertine again.

But Albertine was keeping mum. 'Mum's the word,' she said inscrutably, and she smiled a secret goosey smile again.

Chapter Six

Then one morning, Captain was looking out of his stable after his breakfast, when he saw that Egbert had vanished again.

No-one could find him anywhere. All day long they looked but they still couldn't find him.

At last they went to tell Old Farmer
Rafferty the bad news.

We've lost him again, we've lost Egbert!

But instead of saddling Captain and
going out to look for him, Old
Farmer Rafferty just leant on his
spade and laughed and laughed.

Why don't
you have a
look through
my sitting-
room window?

POW

zip

Jigger got there first.

'Oh yes he can,' laughed Old
Farmer Rafferty. 'He can and he
has because *he* is a *she*.
Egbert is Egberta,
and she's just had
two lovely kids.'

And they all peered in at the window. There was Egberta lying out on the sofa, a cushion under her head, with her two little kids beside her.

That evening, Farmer Farley brought Billy, his billygoat over to Farmer Rafferty's to see his kids.

'It's my Egberta who's the clever one, bless her,' said Farmer Rafferty.

'I'd say they're both clever,' said Farmer Farley.

Meanwhile, Billy chewed the paint off the window and Egberta chewed the sofa, and both of them looked very happy indeed.

Chapter Seven

Out on the pond, Upside and Down came up for a breather. 'Anything new happened?' they asked.

'Not me,' Albertine smiled. 'Egberta. She's the one that's kidding. It'll be nice to have some real kids around won't it children?'

She cuddled her goslings under
her wings, including the one with
the trotters. 'Do you want a story
to send you to sleep?' And of
course they did.

The night came down, the moon
came up and everyone slept on
Mudpuddle Farm.